The Go-cart Team

As told by **Amy Keystone**
to **David Keystone**

Photographs by Bill Thomas

Illustrations by Rae Dale and Nathan Jurevicius

PM Nonfiction

Emerald

U.S. Edition © 2013 Houghton Mifflin Harcourt Publishing Company
125 High Street
Boston, MA 02110
www.hmhco.com

Text © 2001 David Keystone
Photographs © 2001 Cengage Learning Australia Pty Limited
Illustrations © 2001 Cengage Learning Australia Pty Limited
Originally published in Australia by Cengage Learning Australia

18   1957   18
26516

Text: David Keystone
Photographs: Bill Thomas
Printed in China by 1010 Printing International Ltd

The Go-cart Team
ISBN 978 0 76 357454 3

Contents

Introducing Amy—That's Me!

My name is Amy Keystone.
I am nearly ten years old.

Tina

Mansor

Me!!

Ming-En

Yesterday, my friends Mansor, Ming-En, Tina, and I walked by the Greenmount Community Center. Tina looked at the bulletin board and saw something exciting. "Look at this!" she said. "We could do this. It would be a lot of fun."

The Greenmount Festival

Design and make your own go-cart,

so you can be in

The Go-cart Race!

When: Sunday, September 24

Time: 11:00 AM

At: Greenmount Lake

"How do you build a go-cart? Where would you start?" asked Ming-En.

I said, "My dad can help. He has a workshop and he builds lots of things from wood and metals."

Mansor's mom, Mrs. Walipoor, owns a bicycle shop, and Mansor said he knew she would love to help. "Mom could help with wheels and other parts from her bicycle shop," he added.

We were ready to build a go-cart for the race. This is my diary of how we get our go-cart on track. We have a lot to learn!

Starting Out

Today we spoke to my dad at his workshop. He asked us what we wanted to build. Tina suggested that the go-cart should be as light as possible, so that we can push it easily.

"Good thinking," said Dad. "I suggest that you work together." He said that it would be best to draw or make a model for our go-cart before we actually build it.

"Ming-En, you're really good at drawing," said Mansor. "Remember those great race cars you drew in class?"

Ming-En blushed. "Yes," he said nervously.

"We could give you our ideas, and you could draw them," Tina said.

Ming-En smiled and said, "Okay, I'll try."

"When you've agreed on a design, bring it to me, and we'll discuss which materials would be best to use," said Dad.

What a challenge!

Some of our designs.

Week 2

Our Favorite Design

This is Ming-En's drawing of the go-cart design that we all like the best.

Now we have to choose a name. These are some of our suggestions:

Lightning

 Road Hog

 Flash

 Mean Machine

Blitz

Full Speed

We showed Dad our go-cart design. He was impressed! He explained that we now had to look at how our design would be used to actually build a go-cart.

"Where do you think we should start?" asked Dad.

"Probably with the frame," said Ming-En.

Ming-En explained that the frame is a structure that supports the other parts of the go-cart.

Here is Ming-En's drawing of the frame from a bird's-eye view. Can you see what shape the frame makes?

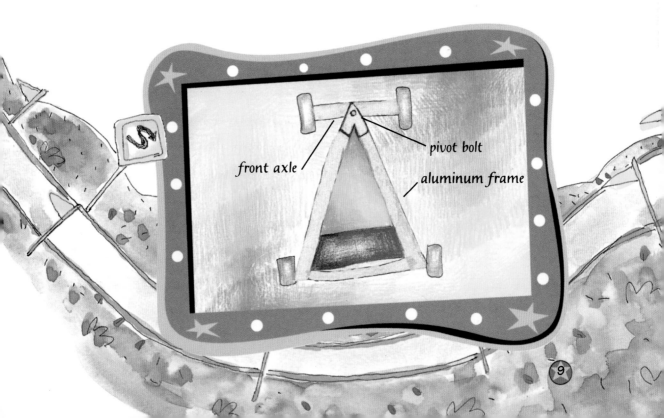

pivot bolt

front axle

aluminum frame

"Do you think that the shape of the frame could make a difference in the strength of the go-cart?" Dad asked.

I wasn't sure, but Tina said that in her class they had made and tested the strength of different shapes. She said they had discovered that triangular shapes are stronger than square shapes.

Here is a list of the parts and materials we need for our go-cart.

saw
wood
electric drill
aluminum tubing
screwdriver
steel bolts, nuts & washers
wheels with bearings
wrench
rope

Week 3

Building Begins

Today we started building! During the week we'd gathered all the parts, materials, and tools on our list. This morning we took them to Dad's workshop.

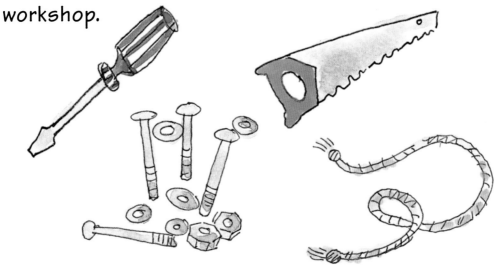

It was a little confusing with so many parts, so we asked Dad a lot of questions. Ming-En asked why the wheels need ball-bearings. Mansor said his mom had explained that bearings help make the wheels turn smoothly by reducing friction.

I asked why we were using aluminum tubing. Dad told us that aluminum is a light, sturdy metal. Using aluminum would make the go-cart lighter. The lighter we make the cart, the less energy we will need to push it.

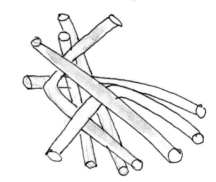

These answers helped us to build the go-cart the way we wanted it. Dad cut the aluminum tubing and drilled some holes for bolts. Then we started to bolt various parts together.

We need to send some of the aluminum tubing to be curved by a pipe bender. That part will be bolted onto the back to act as a pushbar.

Week 4

Hard Work!

Saturday

The aluminum tubing is back from the pipe bender, so we can put our go-cart together!

Here are all the **parts** for the go-cart.

But we've discovered a small problem. Today, Ming-En bravely asked, "What are we going to call our go-cart?" Each of us replied—but with a different name! We burst out laughing.

We each have a name we like, but none of us agree. So, we haven't decided yet.

Making a go-cart is hard work. We all had separate jobs: I checked the seat belt, Tina put the wheels on, Ming-En checked that all the bolts were secure, and Mansor attached the rope to the front axle.

We are almost finished. I can see myself sitting in the driver's seat. Tomorrow, we will plan our training schedule.

Sunday

This morning we met again at Dad's workshop. Mansor had prepared a list of safety gear we need for training. We need:

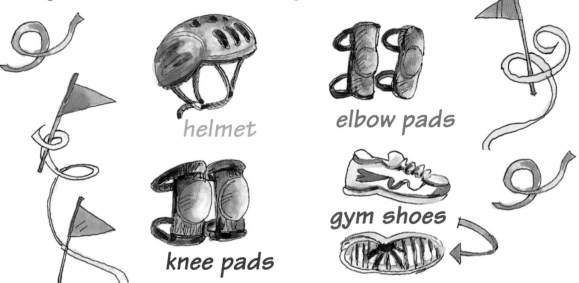

helmet

elbow pads

knee pads

gym shoes

Tina suggested that we have our first training session at the school basketball court. Basketball season hasn't begun yet, so the court will be free. The surface of the court is asphalt and flat, perfect for training.

Ming-En said that the park would be good for future sessions. The park has paths where we can practice our turns.

I suggested we have a practice session at Greenmount Lake.

Later today, we put the finishing touches on our go-cart, and Tina sat in the driver's seat. We are really looking forward to riding in our go-cart.

The race organizers said we are no. 37!

We've also thought of some more names:

Tornado

Spitfire

Flash

Superstar

Jet

Twister

Test Runs

Saturday

Today, Tina, Mansor, and Ming-En pushed me all the way from the workshop to the basketball court. It was fun.

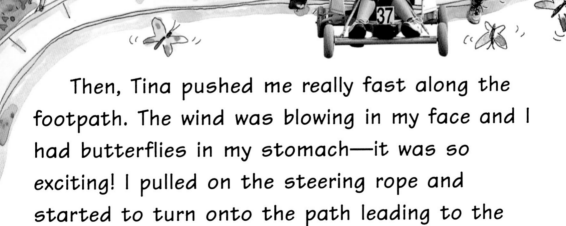

Then, Tina pushed me really fast along the footpath. The wind was blowing in my face and I had butterflies in my stomach—it was so exciting! I pulled on the steering rope and started to turn onto the path leading to the basketball court.

"Go for it, Tina!" I said.

Suddenly, a shaggy dog ran onto the path in front of me. Luckily, I swerved just in time and missed the dog. But the go-cart, Tina, and I went straight into a bush.

Ming-En and Mansor caught up to us shouting, "Amy! Tina! Are you all right?"

Fortunately, the seat belt had held me safely in the go-cart. Tina scrambled out of the bush, unhurt.

Mansor said, "I've got a good idea. Let's call our go-cart Shaggy Dog!" We all smiled, but we knew that wasn't the right name.

Luckily, the go-cart wasn't damaged and the rest of our training session went smoothly.

Sunday

Today we practiced in the park. Tina drove carefully around the walking path while Mansor pushed. As they headed down the path toward the duck pond, the cart started to go really fast. Mansor let go of the go-cart, shouting, "Try out the brake!"

Tina tried the brake. It didn't work! Tina and the go-cart went straight into the pond. She laughed, undid her seat belt, and waded through the shallow water. "Help! My shoes are full of water!"

Poor Tina!

Ming-En laughed, "Maybe we should call the cart Tidal Wave!" That made us really laugh, but again we knew it wasn't the right name for our go-cart.

After drying off the go-cart, we used a wrench to secure the bolt, washer, and nut that keep the handbrake in place. Later, Dad said that we must always check nuts and bolts before and after every practice session.

I think that's good advice!

Meeting the Competition

Today we practiced at Greenmount Lake with some other teams. We nervously eyed the other teams' vehicles. The other teams looked at ours. I think that they were just as excited and nervous as we were. But, of course, we all tried to act as though we weren't nervous at all!

This is one of the carts we saw at Greenmount Lake.

The practice went really well. In fact, we worked so well as a team today that it gave us the idea for the name—Team Spirit! We want everyone to know that working together as a team is important to us.

This is Team Spirit!

If you look up the word "spirit" in the dictionary, you'll find it means boldness, courage, fearlessness. This is just the way we feel.

The Night Before

Today, Tina, Mansor, Ming-En, and I checked every detail on Team Spirit. We all laughed a lot, but I think we are nervous.

My stomach feels knotted up, and I'm not hungry. Mom said that this is my body's way of preparing for an important event. Sometimes I feel calm, other times I feel a little scared.

I think Tina, Mansor, and Ming-En feel the same way—maybe it's called "Team Spirit."

Tomorrow's the big day.

Race Day

Team Spirit is looking good!
It's going to be close!

Last night, I dreamed of crossing
the finish line. Out in the crowd
I could hear someone calling my name,
"Amy, Amy ..." But it was just Mom
waking me up—"Time to get up. Race Day!"

I'm feeling even more nervous than yesterday.
I could hardly eat my breakfast.

Well, I have to go now. I've packed all my
safety gear, and Dad's put the go-cart
in the back of his car. We've got to meet
the rest of the team at ten o'clock.

I'll finish writing this tonight—after the race.

Go, Team Spirit!